Dear Parent:

Congratulations! Your child is taking the first steps on an exciting journey. The destination? Independent reading!

STEP INTO READING® will help your child get there. The program offers books at five levels that accompany children from their first attempts at reading to reading success. Each step includes fun stories, fiction and nonfiction, and colorful art. There are also Step into Reading Sticker Books, Step into Reading Math Readers, and Step into Reading Phonics Readers— a complete literacy program with something to interest every child.

Learning to Read, Step by Step!

Ready to Read **Preschool–Kindergarten**
• big type and easy words • rhyme and rhythm • picture clues
For children who know the alphabet and are eager to begin reading.

Reading with Help **Preschool–Grade 1**
• basic vocabulary • short sentences • simple stories
For children who recognize familiar words and sound out new words with help.

Reading on Your Own **Grades 1–3**
• engaging characters • easy-to-follow plots • popular topics
For children who are ready to read on their own.

Reading Paragraphs **Grades 2–3**
• challenging vocabulary • short paragraphs • exciting stories
For newly independent readers who read simple sentences with confidence.

Ready for Chapters **Grades 2–4**
• chapters • longer paragraphs • full-color art
For children who want to take the plunge into chapter books but still like colorful pictures.

STEP INTO READING® is designed to give every child a successful reading experience. The grade levels are only guides. Children can progress through the steps at their own speed, developing confidence in their reading, no matter what their grade.

Remember, a lifetime love of reading starts with a single step!

For Karen
—B.B.

For Sidney
—C.S.

Text copyright © 1965, 1990 by Barbara Brenner. Illustrations copyright © 1990 by Catherine Siracusa. All rights reserved under International and Pan-American Copyright Conventions. Published in the United States by Random House Children's Books, a division of Random House, Inc., New York, and simultaneously in Canada by Random House of Canada Limited, Toronto. Originally published in 1965 as a Borzoi Book by Alfred A. Knopf, an imprint of Random House, Inc., New York.

www.stepintoreading.com

Educators and librarians, for a variety of teaching tools, visit us at
www.randomhouse.com/teachers

Library of Congress Cataloging-in-Publication Data
Brenner, Barbara.
Beef stew / by Barbara Brenner ; illustrated by Catherine Siracusa.
  p.   cm. — (Step into reading. A step 2 book)
SUMMARY: When his friends decline to come over for a beef stew dinner, Nicky feels bad until a surprise visitor shows up.
ISBN 0-394-85046-7 (trade) — ISBN 0-394-95046-1 (lib. bdg.)
[1. Dinners and dining—Fiction.]   I. Siracusa, Catherine, ill.   II. Title.
III. Series: Step into reading. Step 2 book.   PZ7.B7518Be 2004   [E]—dc21   2002153029

Printed in the United States of America   30 29 28 27 26 25 24 23 22 21

STEP INTO READING, RANDOM HOUSE, and the Random House colophon are registered trademarks of Random House, Inc.

STEP INTO READING® 2 STEP

Beef Stew

By Barbara Brenner
Illustrated by Catherine Siracusa

Random House New York

When Nicky woke up,
he smelled something good.
What was that good smell?

It was beef stew!
"I am making lots of stew,"
said his mother.
"Would you like to ask
a friend for supper?"

"Yes!" Nicky shouted.
He ran off to school
to find a friend—
a friend who liked beef stew.

At school Nicky saw Alec.
Alec was his best friend.
"Can you come for supper?"
asked Nicky.

"Sorry," said Alec.

"I have to go to the dentist."

At lunch Nicky went to sit
with Carla.
"Can you come for supper?
It's beef stew."

Carla shook her head.

"I like hot dogs.

I like burgers.

I like pizza.

But I do not like beef stew!"

Later Nicky went
to the library.
Mr. Blake found
just the right book for him.

So Nicky asked Mr. Blake
to come for supper.
Mr. Blake was sorry,
but he could not come.
"My family is going
to eat out tonight."

On the way home
Nicky looked for a friend
to come for supper.

But he did not find anyone—
anyone who liked beef stew.

Nicky turned the corner.
There was a friend!
"Hi, Officer Gabel,"
Nicky shouted.

"Can you come for supper?"
asked Nicky.
"It's beef stew."
But Officer Gabel
could not come.
"It's my birthday.
There's a party
at the station tonight."

"Happy birthday,"
said Nicky.

He headed down the street.

Nicky saw the garbage man.
But the garbage man
never said hello.
He was not a friend.
And Nicky did not ask him
for supper.

Now Nicky was almost home.
And he felt sad.
He kicked a pebble
down the street.

"No one wants to come
for supper tonight.
No one wants to eat beef stew,"
Nicky said to himself.

"Boy! Do you look sad,"

someone said.

Nicky looked up.

It was Mr. Cone.

"Maybe this will cheer you up."

Mr. Cone handed Nicky
a post card.

Nicky read the post card.
He started jumping
up and down.
"Hooray!"

"Bye, Mr. Cone!"

Nicky called.

Nicky ran all through town,
past the police station,
past the garbage truck,
past his school.

Nicky ran all the way
to the train station.
A train was pulling in.
People got off.

Nicky saw her right away.

He rushed up to her.

His grandma hugged him.
"What a surprise!"
she said.
"I see
you got my post card."

And that is how
Nicky brought a friend home
for supper.
A friend who liked beef stew!